Starfish Bay® Children's Books
An imprint of Starfish Bay Publishing
www.starfishbaypublishing.com

THE MONOLOGUE OF MONSTER

© Grace Suen, 2020
ISBN 978-1-76036-143-3
First Published 2021
Printed in China

Sincere thanks to Elyse Williams from Starfish Bay Children's Books for her creative efforts in preparing this edition for publication.

Also by Grace Suen

The Monologue of Monster

Retold and Illustrated by
Grace Suen

When I first opened my eyes, I saw a messy, dirty, and strange room.

I walked around. I felt cold and confused.

I left the strange house and wandered around outside. It was a stormy night. I felt hungry and thirsty. I was overwhelmed by various noises, howling, hooting and chirping. I was flooded by different smells of the soil, grass and flowers.

Food was scarce, so I often spent days searching. One day, I arrived at a wonderful village with clean cottages and tidy yards. I peered into one of the windows and saw soup and roasted vegetables sitting on the table inside. The family inside noticed my presence. I was greeted by shrieking as they fled from the cottage. The whole village was roused. Some villagers fled, while others attacked me until I was bruised and battered.

I fled toward the open fields and came across a farm with a cottage. I took refuge in the small wooden shed behind it. I stayed in the shed, only venturing out to occasionally pick apples from nearby trees. Days turned into weeks, and I became familiar with the family who lived there. It was home to a lovely young girl named Agatha, her hardworking brother, Felix, and their caring father, Alfred.

One day, while I was in the shed,
I noticed that a window to the
cottage had been patched with
planks of wood.

Between the planks was a miniscule gap that I could just see through.

I saw a small room that was clean and had little furniture. The girl knitted at the table, while her father sat by the fireplace. The brother had just returned home with a sack of potatoes.

The old man picked up an instrument and played a lilting melody. It was a lovely sound! They looked like a perfect family. I began to understand what love meant.

I admired the perfect family. But whenever I saw my reflection in a pool of water, I was horrified and disgusted. I looked terrifying compared to the perfect family.

I looked like a monster.

But I enjoyed my routine. In the early hours of the morning, I did the chores that I had seen the young man doing outside. During the day, when the family was awake, I rested while observing them. When they went to bed, I gathered food and firewood for them.

To the family, it seemed an invisible force had performed their chores. I heard them utter "Wonderful" and "Good spirit" in astonishment.

Spring came quickly. The weather was fine, the sky void of clouds. The family sat outside, enjoyed the weather and chatted. Laughter rang through the air. I longed to join them.

One night, I discovered some books in the forest. I had learned some language while living in the shed, so when the family was busy, I occupied myself by reading the books.

When winter came, I realized I had been in this world for almost
a year. I longed for the family's acceptance and kindness.
One day, only the father was at home, so I knocked on the door.

"Who is it?" he called out.

"I'm… I'm the one who's been helping your family." The father
welcomed me in.

I hesitated, worried about his reaction.

The father got a clearer look at me. "Who… what are you?" he asked slowly.

I relaxed. He didn't cast me away as other people had in the past.

"I'm… a monster," I said sadly. I explained all that had happened to me.

Slowly, the fear left his face, and he shook his head. "No, you're different, but you're no monster. You have a kind heart."

At that moment, I heard footsteps. Felix and Agatha were back. When they entered, the father said to them, "Don't be afraid. He is our friend."

Felix and Agatha's fear slowly disappeared. They smiled gratefully when they found out I had been helping them.

They knew I had nowhere to go, so they offered to let me continue living in the shed.

"But let me fix the shed up first," said Felix. "It's hardly a proper home right now."

I had finally found a home.